This book belongs to:

The Oklahoma SCRANIMAL

The Oklahoma SCRANIMAL

Written By
Larry Derryberry

TATE PUBLISHING & *Enterprises*

Published by Tate Publishing & Enterprises, LLC
127 E. Trade Center Terrace | Mustang, Oklahoma 73064 USA
1.888.361.9473 | www.tatepublishing.com

Tate Publishing is committed to excellence in the publishing industry. The company reflects the philosophy established by the founders, based on Psalms 68:11,
"The Lord gave the word and great was the company of those who published it."

Book design copyright © 2007 by Tate Publishing, LLC. All rights reserved.
Illustrations, Cover Design, and Interior Design by Kristen Polson
Original Concept Illustrations by Gale Derryberry
Cover photo of Gov. Brad Henry by Tom Flora

Published in the United States of America

ISBN: 978-1-6024731-8-8
1. Juvenile Fiction   2. Animals: Farm Animals
3. Oklahoma
07.08.08

Dedicated to our grandchildren

Tristan Michael Prentice

Andrew Robert Derryberry

Olivia Anne Derryberry

Ava Gale Prentice

The Oklahoma storm clouds were rollin'
at Papa Derryberry's farm,

when a big tornado came out of the sky
and picked up the big red barn.

Inside were five farm animals
eating breakfast that summer morn.
A cow and a horse, a sheep and a pig
and a duck were caught up in that storm.

The **COW** said, "I think we're moo-o-ving."
The sheep said, "This **ba-a-arn's** hit ba-a-ad."
The **horse** said, "Let's call the neigh-eigh-bors.
It's the **worst** tornado we've ever had."

The little pig never stopped eating.
He said, "It will be oink, oink, oin-kay."
The duck said, "I don't have to flap my wings.
This barn is quackly, quackly flying away."

The barn was tossed and turned and twisted like a Jell-o man with rubber legs,

and the five farm animals were stirred together like a skillet full of scrambled eggs.

There were horns and hide and teeth and tails,
and when the storm was finally done,

where five animals used to be,
now there was only one.

It was a "Scranimal!"
Five scrambled animals
inside of the big red barn.
It was a "Scranimal!"
Five scrambled animals
on Papa Derryberry's farm.

He had two horns on the top of his head,
and his nose was a short, pink snout.
He had webbed feet at the end of his legs,
and a curly tail he wiggled about.

He had fleecy wool from his head to his toe.
He was white with patches of black.
He had a cow bell hung around his neck,
and a saddle strapped on his back.

He made a funny noise when he started to speak—
it was part "Quack" and part "Moo."
You occasionally heard a "Neigh" and a "Baaaa,"
and even an "Oink, oink" or two.

He said, "I love oats and ears of corn,
and an occasional bale of hay.
But most of all I love the pasture grass,
and I roll in it every day."

Papa Derryberry had a worry.
Just what was he to do?
Should he take his lovable Scranimal
to the metropolitan ZOO?

He knew from his smile and those big white teeth
that he was happy in that big red barn.
So he decided he could spend the rest of his life
on Papa Derryberry's farm!

THE END

e|LIVE

listen|imagine|view|experience

AUDIO BOOK DOWNLOAD INCLUDED WITH THIS BOOK!

In your hands you hold a complete digital entertainment package. Besides purchasing the paper version of this book, this book includes a free download of the audio version of this book. Simply use the code listed below when visiting our website. Once downloaded to your computer, you can listen to the book through your computer's speakers, burn it to an audio CD or save the file to your portable music device (such as Apple's popular iPod) and listen on the go!

How to get your free audio book digital download:

1. Visit www.tatepublishing.com and click on the e|LIVE logo on the home page.
2. Enter the following coupon code:
   af78-8843-235f-f94d-352f-45a9-f80b-d827
3. Download the audio book from your e|LIVE digital locker and begin enjoying your new digital entertainment package today!